STORIES OF
FRIENDSHIP

SOCIAL EMOTIONAL LIBRARY

Published in the United States of America by Cherry Lake Publishing
Ann Arbor, Michigan
www.cherrylakepublishing.com

Content Adviser: Satta Sarmah Hightower, www.sattasarmah.com
Reading Adviser: Marla Conn MS, Ed., Literacy specialist, Read-Ability, Inc.

Photo Credits: ©interstid/Shutterstock Images, cover, 1; ©Rawpixel.com/Shutterstock Images, 5; ©Wikimedia, 7;
©Wikimedia, 8; ©Andrei Nekrassov/Shutterstock Images, 11; ©Genvessel/Flickr, 12; ©s_bukley/Shutterstock Images, 15;
©malingering/Wikimedia, 16; ©catwalker/Shutterstock Images, 17; ©Natursports/Shutterstock Images, 18; ©tristan tan/
Shutterstock Images, 21; ©Loreta Conte/Flickr, 22; ©hepingting/Flickr, 25; ©Monkey Business Images/Shutterstock
Images, 27; ©Blend Images/Shutterstock Images, 28

Library of Congress Cataloging-in-Publication Data
Names: Colby, Jennifer, 1971- author.
Title: Stories of friendship / by Jennifer Colby.
Description: Ann Arbor : Cherry Lake Publishing, [2018] | Series: Social emotional library |
    Audience: Grade 4 to 6. | Includes bibliographical references and index.
Identifiers: LCCN 2017033503 | ISBN 9781534107427 (hardcover) | ISBN 9781534109407 (pdf) |
    ISBN 9781534108417 (pbk.) | ISBN 9781534120396 (hosted ebook)
Subjects: LCSH: Friendship—Juvenile literature.
Classification: LCC BF575.F66 C635 2018 | DDC 177/.62—dc23
LC record available at https://lccn.loc.gov/2017033503

Cherry Lake Publishing would like to acknowledge the work of The Partnership for 21st Century Learning.
Please visit www.p21.org for more information.

Printed in the United States of America
Corporate Graphics

ABOUT THE AUTHOR

Jennifer Colby is a school librarian in Michigan. Though she writes books alone,
she still has great friendships with other authors.

TABLE OF CONTENTS

CHAPTER 1

What Is Friendship?

Do you have people in your life who you are close to? Maybe they are people who are the same age as you or have the same interests and hobbies. Friends are people you can talk to and share your life with. Friendship exists in many forms. Some friendships last for many years, while some may only last for a few hours. There have been many famous friendships in history, but there are some you may have never heard about.

Friends listen to and respect each other.

CHAPTER 2

The Christmas Truce

Friends can be found in the unlikeliest of places, even on the battlefield. Have you ever fought with someone? Did you make up? What if you made up but were forced to go back to fighting each other? That is exactly what happened during World War I (WWI).

From 1914 to 1918, a war involving almost every country in the world took place. WWI was called the "war to end all wars." Two opposing **alliances** between countries formed, and promises were made to protect and defend each other if threatened. The two groups of countries already distrusted each other, and the war was sparked by the **assassination** of Archduke Franz Ferdinand, the heir to the throne of Austria-Hungary. A Serbian **nationalist** killed the archduke, and Austria-Hungary

German and British soldiers play soccer, also known as football, together.

reacted by declaring war on Serbia. When the allied countries responded to this **declaration**, World War I began.

A major area of fighting happened along the western front in Europe. The front stretched 440 miles (708 kilometers) from the Swiss border to the North Sea. At the beginning of the war it was the main point of battle, and it remained that way until the war ended. Hundreds of battles were fought along the front for four long years, and there were 17 million deaths during the war.

This cross in Belgium marks the site of the Christmas Truce.

In December of the first year of the war, a series of unofficial **cease-fires** occurred along the front. Fighting up to that point had been rough. British troops battled against German troops along miles of **trenches** that were dug and then **fortified** with **barbed wire**, machine guns, and **artillery**.

During the week before Christmas, German troops put up trees and candles in their trenches and celebrated the season by singing Christmas carols. British troops responded by singing carols of their own. The shared singing encouraged the soldiers to climb out of their trenches to exchange prisoners and bury their dead. In some cases, enemy troops even shared meals and played soccer with each other.

Approximately 10,000 British and German soldiers scattered along the front put down their weapons and crossed the battle lines to wish each other a Merry Christmas. A British soldier wrote, "We are having the most extraordinary Christmas Day imaginable. A … truce exists between us and our friends in front. The funny thing is it only seems to exist in this part of the battle line—on our right and left, we can all hear them firing away as cheerfully as ever. ... Here the agreement—all on their own— came to be made that we should not fire at each other until after midnight tonight."

During Christmas 1914, men at war found it in their hearts to put aside their differences, find common ground, and build friendships, if only for a short time. In this case, it was the celebration of a shared holiday that encouraged goodwill to others.

CHAPTER 3

J. R. R. Tolkien and C. S. Lewis

Are you and your best friend both good at the same thing?
Maybe you are both talented at drawing, or maybe you play
against each other on the basketball court. Sometimes it is hard
to stay friends when you are also competing against each other.
This is called a rivalry. A rivalry can be friendly, but sometimes it
is not. Two famous British authors proved that a strong friendship
can be built and maintained even through years of competition.

Author John Ronald Reuel (J. R. R.) Tolkien, born in 1892,
wrote the *The Hobbit* and *The Lord of the Rings* trilogy. Author
Clive Staples (C. S.) Lewis, born in 1898, wrote *The Chronicles
of Narnia*. They met in 1926 while teaching at Oxford University
in England. They were similar in many ways. Both men ignored

Tolkien was a professor of English Language and Literature at Merton College, where he finished writing *The Lord of the Rings* in 1948.

politics and news, and both turned their backs on modern society—neither one of them drove a car.

But it was their shared interest in myths and storytelling that brought them together. Before Tolkien and Lewis were published authors, they belonged to a writing club where authors met to read and discuss each other's work. They soon found that they were the only two authors interested in the **fantasy** genre— other club members wrote about more serious subjects. Tolkien and Lewis both agreed that fantasy literature, though interesting to them, had yet to have anything written that was worth reading.

A statue in Belfast, Northern Ireland, shows Lewis entering the wardrobe from the *Chronicles of Narnia*.

So they decided to write their own fantasy books, and they became each other's first readers.

The two men shared a similar past—they had lost their parents and both had fought in World War I. The two bonded over their unhappy experiences. Tolkien and Lewis filled their uncommon **escapist** stories with fantastical creatures, wizards, and magic, things considered **frivolous** by other writers. They became each other's greatest support. Tolkien wrote of Lewis, "The unpayable **debt** that I owe to him was not 'influence' as it is ordinarily understood, but sheer encouragement." They not only read each other's works, Lewis helped to publicize Tolkien's *The Lord of the Rings*.

Combined, their works have had more than 300 million copies printed, have been translated into 39 languages, and have been made into films earning more than $6.4 billion. Lewis died in 1963. In a letter to his daughter only four days after Lewis's death, Tolkien remembered their friendship fondly as something they had always carried with them. This close, supportive friendship helped both writers to create some of the most popular stories of all time.

CHAPTER 4

Lionel Messi and Kobe Bryant

Friends can have a lot in common. You can be on the same team or play in the same musical group. Making friends is easy when you see each other all the time. But sometimes friends meet just because they are each amazingly talented and at the top of their game. It seems like it would be difficult for people who play different sports on the other side of the world from each other to develop a friendship. But soccer star Lionel Messi and basketball star Kobe Bryant have shown how this is possible.

They were introduced to each other in Los Angeles by a mutual friend. Bryant was told that 17-year-old Messi would become the greatest soccer player of all time. Thirteen years later, both men are now considered to be among the best athletes ever to play their **respective** sports. "We're the same, Messi and I,"

Bryant is a whopping 6 feet and 6 inches (198.12 cm) tall.

Bryant played basketball for 20 years with the Los Angeles Lakers.

Bryant said. "As people, in the way that we speak, we are different … but we are the same in the love that we feel for our sports."

Born in 1987 in Argentina, Lionel Messi plays forward for the Spanish FC Barcelona club and the Argentine national soccer team. Considered one of the greatest soccer players of all time, Messi is the only player in history to have won five FIFA Ballon d'Or awards for being the world's best male soccer player that year. During his career, he has led his teams to many titles. With Messi, Argentina titled in the under-20 World Cup and FC Barcelona earned titles in the Spanish Super Cup.

Messi holds a FIFA Ballon d'Or award.

Members of the FC Barcelona club soccer team celebrate Messi's goal.

Born in 1978, Bryant is a retired NBA basketball player. He played for the Los Angeles Lakers for his entire professional career, and so he holds the record for playing the most seasons for the same team. Bryant won five NBA Championships with the Lakers, was an 18-time All Star, and led the NBA in scoring during two of his seasons.

Their cross-cultural friendship is famous. They have filmed commercials together for Turkish Airlines that display their competitive spirits. In one commercial, they have a selfie competition that takes them around the world. In another commercial, they **vie** for a young boy's autograph by trying to outdo each other with their skills at athletics, building playing card houses, and even making balloon animals.

Both men reached the peak of their sports, but still appreciate each other's accomplishments and talents. When Bryant retired from basketball, Messi was one of thousands to send good wishes. "It's always sad to hear when a sportsman is retiring. But Kobe Bryant will always be in the history books as one of the greatest," said Messi of his friend. Bryant and Messi showed how great friendships can grow because of mutual respect and admiration.

Are You a Good Friend?

How many friends do you have? Do you think that the more friends you have, the better friend you are? Whether you have one friend or 100 friends, if you have a relationship built with trust, respect, and understanding, then you are a good friend.

CHAPTER 5

Suryia the Orangutan and Roscoe the Bluetick Coonhound

Do you have friends that are not like you? Sometimes we make friends with people who don't live in the same town, state, or even country that we do. Sometimes we make friends with people who are not our age. But friendships can also form between different species. Examples of unlikely animal pairings from around the world include a gorilla and kitten, a rhinoceros and a goat, and even a rat and a cat. A very special friendship formed in 2008 between an orangutan and a dog.

Suryia, a male orangutan, and Roscoe, a male bluetick coonhound, met at an animal preserve in Myrtle Beach, South Carolina. Roscoe had followed rescue workers home one day, and Suryia—who was already at the preserve and sad after losing

Before meeting Roscoe, Suryia used to live in the preserve with his parents.

his parents—walked over to the thin stray dog. They immediately began to play. This was unusual because dogs are normally afraid of primates. Suryia and Roscoe have been **inseparable** ever since.

Native to Indonesia and Malaysia, orangutans live in the rainforests, spending most of their time in the trees searching for fruit. They are extremely smart and have been observed creating and using tools to get seeds from fruit, to dig out insects from trees, and to communicate. Orangutans are not very social, and they prefer to spend most of their time alone. However, Suryia

Sometimes Suryia slips Roscoe his monkey biscuits.

acts as an adoptive parent to rescued primates in the preserve.
Bluetick coonhounds are extremely active. Bred as hunting dogs,
they have a huge amount of energy and are happiest when they
are swimming, running, or playing.

Suryia and Roscoe spend a few hours together each day wrestling,
swimming, and hanging out. Suryia even takes Roscoe on walks.
He holds Roscoe's leash and scoots and flips along behind his
canine friend. Sometimes both animals take a ride together on
the back of one of the preserve's rescue elephants. Their unlikely

friendship has been reported in newspapers around the world and on television, and there is even a picture book written about it.

We don't always know what animals are thinking, but this unusual friendship between two different species shows us that animals are capable of great feeling and understanding. Though they would have never connected in the wild, special factors brought Suryia and Roscoe together. Now they enjoy each other's company and are happy spending time with each other doing what friends do.

Friendship in the Workplace

Do you have a person you can talk to about almost anything? Friends are great to have during your career, and they can help you be successful at work. They can provide another point of view if you need advice about something that's bothering you. Friends can also help you with something you're working on. Having friends is a lot of fun, and it can help you become more cooperative and understanding of people's differences.

CHAPTER 6

Fifth Graders Stand Up for Bullied Classmate

James Willmert has a **learning disability**. His new friends notice that he sometimes has a hard time tying his shoes or opening up potato chip bags at lunch. But they help him when he needs it. Because of a **neurological disorder**, some children with learning disabilities can have trouble reading, writing, reasoning, recalling, or organizing information. Learning disabilities are not uncommon, but they can be helped by things like a change in routine, extra time to finish an assignment, or reading aloud.

A good friend helps when you're being bullied.

Going to school at Franklin Elementary in Mankato, Minnesota, James complained a lot about recess to his mother. During fifth grade, fellow students saw James being bullied by classmates on the playground. The bullies were not being physically harmful, but one friend said, "They were using him and taking advantage of him, because he's easier to pick on, and it's just not right."

Jack Pemble, Jake Burgess, Gus Gartzke, Tyler Jones, and Landon Kopischke decided that the best way to stop the bullies from picking on James was to be his friend. They invited James to their lunch table and included him in their games at recess. They wanted to prevent him having contact with the bullies. While getting to know James, his new friends asked him what kind of sports video games he owned. James admitted that not only did he not own any games, he didn't even own a gaming system. His friends decided that they wanted to do something nice for him, so they combined their money and (with help from their parents) bought James a new PlayStation 3 and some video games.

This act itself was special. But when the boys came over to deliver their present, James's mother appreciated them even more because it was the first time any friends had ever come over to play with James. Now, she has noticed that James is excited for

The cafeteria can be scary if you don't know who to sit with.

Friends can play games cooperatively and competitively.

recess and barely gets a chance to finish his lunch before going out to play with his friends. The boys' classroom teacher saw this new friendship and nominated the boys for a Spirit of Youth Award, which was awarded to James and his friends by the Mankato Area Public Schools.

What started as a way to prevent bullying on the playground blossomed into a friendship. James's new friends are amazed at his love of sports—he keeps a notebook with information about more than 600 college teams. One friend thinks "he's an awesome kid to hang out with." James and his friends prove that friendships grow when trust and respect are shown to each other.

What Have You Learned About Friendship?

Friendship can take place in many forms. We usually think that friends have a lot in common, but sometimes they don't. Friendships begin when people trust and respect each other, especially because of a similar interest or experience. Sometimes the unlikeliest of friendships can occur—all it takes is a moment of understanding. Good friends encourage us and support us. They try to make us feel better when we are sad, and they share our joy when we are happy. A strong friendship can triumph over differences of any kind.

Think About It

How Can You Become a Better Friend?

There are many ways to become a better friend, but the most important thing a good friend can do is be a good listener. It helps to have a good friend listen to you when you have a problem or have some exciting news to share. Listen to your friends. You can help them more if you know what they are thinking and how they are feeling.

For More Information

Further Reading

Cummings, Rhoda. *The Survival Guide for Kids with LD*. Minneapolis, MN: Free Spirit Publishing, 2016.

Duriez, Colin. *Tolkien and C. S. Lewis: The Gift of Friendship*. Mahwah, NJ: Paulist Press, 2003.

Ellis, Deborah. *We Want You to Know: Kids Talk About Bullying*. Regina, Saskatchewan: Coteau Books, 2010.

Websites

FC Barcelona—All About Leo Messi
https://www.fcbarcelona.com/lionel-messi
Messi's career is highlighted at the official team site.

History—Christmas Truce of 1914
www.history.com/topics/world-war-i/christmas-truce-of-1914
Learn more about the Christmas Truce of 1914 through videos and speeches.

Nat Geo Wild—Unlikely Animal Friends
http://channel.nationalgeographic.com/wild/unlikely-animal-friends/
Find stories and videos about unlikely animal friends.

NBA—Kobe: 20 Unforgettable Seasons
www.nba.com/kobe-tribute/
This official NBA site highlights Bryant's professional basketball career.

GLOSSARY

alliances (uh-LYE-uhns-iz) agreements to work together for some result, such as protecting each other

artillery (ahr-TIL-uh-ree) large, powerful guns that are mounted on wheels or tracks

assassination (uh-SAS-uh-nay-shun) killing a famous or important person, usually for political reasons

barbed wire (BARBD WYE-ur) twisted strands of wire with sharp points, used for fences

cease-fires (SEES-fye-urz) temporary pauses during a war, usually to allow peace talks to take place

debt (DET) money or something else that someone owes

declaration (dek-luh-RAY-shuhn) the act of making an official statement about something

escapist (ih-SKAYP-ist) a form of entertainment that allows people to forget about the real problems of life

fantasy (FAN-tuh-see) a story with magical or strange characters, places, or events

fortified (FOR-tuh-fyed) strengthened by building walls for protection from attack

frivolous (FRIV-uh-luhs) silly, without any real purpose

inseparable (in-SEP-ur-uh-buhl) not able to be apart from each other

learning disability (LUR-ning dis-uh-BIL-ih-tee) a condition that makes learning a basic skill difficult

nationalist (NASH-uh-nuh-list) a member of a political group with the desire to form an independent nation

neurological disorder (noor-ah-LOJ-ih-kuhl dis-OR-dur) a problem with the nervous system

respective (rih-SPEK-tiv) relating to each one of the things that have been mentioned

trenches (TRENCH-iz) long, narrow holes dug in the ground to be shelters from enemy attack

vie (VYE) to compete with others in an attempt to win something

INDEX